Published by Terence J Goodchild @ Amazon
Createspace

ISBN 9798467275543 (paperback) Amazon

Intro

A witch named Solengena Aristona now Solengena did not like the name her parents had given her they were both gardeners and thought it a good idea to name her after a plant and she could not handle being named after a lowly plant so Solengena decided she would change her name by deed poll but had no idea how to go about it the only thing she could think of was the sorcerer Singasong Sam who lived in Zeb's windy city was he only one who could help her, so off she flew on her broomstick to seek out his help.

A WITCH BY ANY OTHER NAME

By

Terence J Goodchild

Once upon a time in a land far away called far away land there lived a witch called Solengena Aristona now Solengena did not like the name her parents had given her as it reminded her of a certain plant she could not handle being named after a lowly plant so Solengena decided she could change her name by deed poll but had no idea how to go about it.

She thought she would consult the best brain in the land, he was a sorcerer named Singasong Sam and he lived in a place named Zeb's windy city on account of it being windy I think or maybe it was named after the founder Jeremiah Zeb who's wife Matilda made meat pies and mushy peas in her bakery, well work it out yourselves

The next day she set off for Zeb's windy city to see Singasong Sam she had no idea how he was going to help her but would figure it out when she arrived there.

Now in Zeb's windy city confusion reigned, it is not wet, but confused if you get my meaning, it concerned Singasong Sam whether he was any good as a sorcerer or not as the case may be, some of the folks said he was the best damn sorcerer around and others said he could not do any magic even if his life depended on it, which sometimes it did.

There was the time the king lost his voice and Singasong Sam tried to conjure up a potion to relieve the king of his sore throat so he could sing, but it did not work and the king was appearing in the king and him at the country theatre that very night.

When the potion did not work Sam got worried then he had an idea and said to the king

"You pretend to sing just open your mouth and I will sing for you okay."

"What a great idea, but can you sing." The king asked.

"Well put it this way I can sing better than you at this moment in time your majesty, some say I whistle out of tune but like is say at this moment in time what choice do we have."

"Point taken Sam." the king replied.

"Have you just thought of this Sam? The king

asked.

“No its been done before by two goblins that live in the woods called Villanius Mannillius they did it for some talent contest but got found out and were banished to the nothingness never to be heard of again, you have nothing to worry about your majesty, I mean, who is going to question the word or singing of the king, besides your bigger than them, trust me I know what I am doing, and who in their right mind is going to banish you to the nothingness.” Sam smiled well more like a smirk.

*****

All the next day Sam practiced his singing, while he doing this all the birds in the castle grounds heard this noise and came to investigate they gathered on the roof in the gutters in the trees, everywhere they could to find out what it was that made this noise, all around the castle people wandered what had caused this vision.

“Do you think it is the end of the world as we know it?

One of the customers said in the bakers shop.

"No idea." said the baker.

One of the customers named Claude said,

"I remember a long time ago in the village of LA there was this magician named Ilfrid Hatchcock he made a spell and it went wrong and all the birds from villages all over district near LA came and attacked all the people they ate all the crops the farmers had gathered for winter, it was terrible and no one had any idea how to get rid of them."

"So what happened? The baker asked

"Well they sent riders to every town and village to see who could help, and after two weeks they found this man named the piper in a village called Hambling he agreed for a princely sum to rid the all of the birds from the village of LA so the king of LA agreed under duress to pay the piper, so they sent for him, and when he arrived he was all dressed in black.

"What is your name piper? The king asked.

"My name is Jethro your majesty."

"Okay Jethro can you get rid of theses pesky birds?

“Yes your majesty but it will cost you.” Jethro replied.

“How much is the cost? The king asked.

“I want the hand of the fairest maiden in your village, and 20 thousand duckets in gold.”

“You drive a hard bargain sir.” The king replied.

“Well get over it would you like me to leave, I will be back tomorrow at noon.” Jethro left.

*****

“Now the king knew that the fairest maiden in the village was his daughter, but he was not giving her hand to this vagabond, no he had to find someone else, but who then the thought hit him and he fell over, well no he didn’t I just threw that in, on with the story,

“The second most fairest maiden, was the daughter of his general Sir Maurice Biggs but he knew his daughter was betrothed to one of his captains and he was a brave fighter now how was he to outwit Biggs to get his daughter to go with Jethro, So he sent Biggs on a mission to find a left hand screwdriver, so off Biggs went on his trusty steed to find a left hand screwdriver, and then the king sent for Gwendolyn the second fairest maiden, she arrived and the king said.

"Gwendolyn I need to do me a favor."

"What is that my lord? She said.

"We are having trouble with all these birds and need a person to get rid of them."

"You are not thinking I can do that I know my father is a general in the army but I know nothing about war."

"Will you shut up" The King said.

"Cor blimey women I don't know, we need you to go with the piper named Jethro as he is the only one who can help us and he needs the fairest damsel in the village."

"Oh really I am the fairest in the village am I and here is me thinking I am the second fairest in the village."

"Will you shut up, my word you do carry on, we know you are not the fairest and my daughter is but you will have to do as I am not giving my daughter to him." The King said.

"Oh very nice I come second hand hey well let me tell you your majesty you can go and jump." Gwendolyn stood there hands crossed stamping her foot.

"You must obey me I am your king." The king said

"Wait until my father finds out he is not going to be pleased and you know how angry he can get." Gwendolyn still stood there this time hands on hips.

"Okay what if I pay you?

"Okay how much?

"Oh yes you are just like the vagabond Jethro." The king said

"Did you say Jethro the vagabond known as the piper? Gwendolyn asked.

"Yes why have you heard of him? The king said.

"Have I, now we are talking what have I to do tell me tell me please." Gwendolyn gets all excited.

"Well he will get rid of all the birds if he can have the fairest maiden in the village he cannot have my daughter so you will have to do." The king said.

"Well I suppose I will have to do then wont I your majesty when do we meet." She smiled.

"What about your betrothed the captain Eliza Scot what about him, will he not be annoyed at you for forsaking him? The king asked.

"Eliza who I don't know anyone by that name" She smiled.

Oh how fickle some women are the king thought.

"Okay I will arrange for you to meet Jethro tomorrow come to the castle at noon, and dress nice."

"Sorted see you tomorrow your highness." She curtsied and left.

The king sent for his banker Silas who knocked on the door and came in.

"You summoned me my lord?

"Yes Silas do we have 20 thousand duckets in the

bank?

“Of course we do and more.” Silas said.

“Well we need that amount tomorrow to give to Jethro the piper to get rid of all these pesky birds, can you arrange it?

“Yes your majesty how does he want to take it out of the castle? Silas asked.

“I don’t know in bags or something you are the banker why ask me?

“Because you are the king are you not your majesty.”

“Oh yes of course anyway he wants it ask him tomorrow, now go and count it” The king waved his hand to dismiss Silas and sat down while the birds pecked at his window.

*****

The next morning bright and early has he had no sleep with the birds pecked at his window the king summoned Silas again.

“Did you do as I commanded you to do Silas?

"Yes your majesty we have 20 thousand duckets in cases each holding 500 duckets that is 40 cases."

"Yes I can count I am not stupid well where are they?

"In the bank my lord where would they be" Silas looked at the king.

"Oh yes of course I have had no sleep with these pesky birds."

"Yes my lord of course you haven't mind you no one else has either." Silas looked the king.

"Oh yes silly me, now Jethro will be here at noon so you be here as well so he can tell we are serious about getting rid of the birds, now go and prepare."

"Yes my lord." Silas left.

*****

At noon all were assembled in the castle grand ballroom, the king was in his coronation garb with his crown on, Gwendolyn was dressed in her best gown, her hair all done up in curls, Silas was in his best bank clothes and four servants stood in their best clothes all waiting for Jethro to arrive. They waited and waited for a longtime at fifty minutes to one Jethro arrived he swaggered in dressed in his new black suit with tight leggings, Gwendolyn nearly fainted.

“Your majesty you are all waiting for me how nice.”

Jethro sneered.

“Okay Jethro get rid of these pesky birds and this fair maiden is yours to keep.” The king pointed to Gwendolyn who fainted.

“Does she do this all of the time sire? Jethro asked.

“How do I know she is not my daughter” The king replied

“Yes but I am.” Jethro turned to see where the voice was coming from and saw Katrina smiling his heart skipped a beat as she was beautiful.

“What are you doing here my daughter this is no place for you, now go home.” The king ordered to go home.

“No father I am the fairest in the land and I will

stay."

"No you won't he saw me first do as your father says and go home he is mine." Gwendolyn stood there hands on hips.

"We will let Jethro choose who is the fairest in the land." Katrina smirked.

Jethro stood looking at the two women

"I will take them both." He said.

"You cannot do that she is my daughter."

The king shouted

"But Jethro played his flute and the two girls were mesmerized as in a trance and followed the piper and no one could do anything to stop him, mind you he only took one sack of gold as the rest was too heavy for him to carry."

"Great the baker shouted let's find this piper and quickly."

"Why? Claude asked.

"Because he can get rid of all the birds" The baker

said.

“Yes but there is no fair maiden in this city, there is some fair ugly ones but no fair maiden as Katrina was or Gwendolyn,

No all you have to do is tell that silly sorcerer of the kings to stop singing he is practicing for the King and him because the king cannot sing mind you Sam cannot either why he is called sing a song Sam is anyone guess sp all you have to do is tell him to stop singing and all the birds will go.”

“How do you know this? The baker asked.

“A little bird told me, do you know when you throw bread out for them they put it in their ears.” Claude says.

“Why did you not tell us this before? The baker asked.

“Because I had nothing to do and thought I may as well tell you a story.” Claude smiled.

So they all got together and went to the castle and told Sam to stop singing, and would you believe it the birds started to fly away apart from the ones that had bread in their ears but then saw their flock flying away and took the bread out of their ears and followed them into the sky and all was quiet.

“You see I was right.” Claude said.

“You sure are smarty pants.” The baker sneered.

The king heard about Claude and asked the court messenger to go and get him as he wanted to talk to him.

The court messenger went to find Claude but no one knew where he lived so he asked the baker.

“I have no idea he is just a customer of mine and he tells a good story ask in the ale house they know everyone.” The baker replied.

The messenger went to the ale house and went inside.

“Bar do you know a man named Claude as the king wishes to see him?

The barman thought and then thought again and was deep in thought when the messenger shouted

“Well do you or not? This woke up the barman.

“Oh yes Claude, no I don’t never heard of him he never comes in here at all you might ask the local bobby at the bobby station he may know him.”

The messenger stormed out the ale house was quite the barman went back to sleep, the messenger reached the bobby house and went in, there sat a bobby in his bobby uniform and asked the messenger what he wanted.

“Do you know a man named Claude as the king wants to see him?

The bobby thought and then thought again.

“Let me see Claude.” Then he thought again.

“Claude who? He asked.

“I don’t know you fool how many people in this city are called Claude I have no idea what his second name is I only know him as Claude, surely you must have some papers with people’s names on them after all you are the law?

“That is right but don’t call me surely, right lets me look at my papers.’ He started to look through his papers and the messenger waited and waited.

“Right found him he had a bit of a run in with the butcher, he said he told to many stories and threw him out of his shop and Claude threw a brick threw his window and we had to arrest him for causing a mess on the pavement and ruining the butchers chops and steak.” Then he stopped.

“Well where does this Claude live? He shouted at the bobby who then woke up.

“Oh yes er let me see he lives with his mother she is a seamstress and very good I have heard.” The bobby replied then stopped again.

“Hello is there anyone in there where does he live I am not interested in his mother who is a seamstress where do they live?

By now the messenger was getting fed up and angry and thinking these people protect us god help us.

“Yes Fernley cottage off Fernley road number 10.”

“Well thank goodness for that and thanks for making my life ten minutes shorter.” The messenger said angrily and then left.

“You are welcome” the bobby shouted.

*****

So the messenger went around to Fernley road and found Fernley cottage and knocked on the door and waited and waited then he heard this faint noise coming from behind the door then the door opened and an old lady came out.

“Yes what do you want? She asked.

“Could I speak with your son Claude please?

“Why? She asked.

“I am the king’s messenger and have come from the king with this message he wants to see him.”

“Why? She asked again.

What is wrong with the people of this city are they all daft

“I have just told you the king wants to see him.”
“Why? She asked again, now by this time it was getting silly and annoying.

“The king wants to give him a reward.” The

messenger replied.

“Why? She asked again.

“Look tell your son to come to the castle immediately he arrives home, otherwise he will send some solders to kill him okay tell him, now good day.” The messenger walked away

“That should get his attention.”

The messenger arrived back at the castle and went to see the king who was in his throne room checking his throne.

“Your majesty I have left a message with the man named Claude’s mother to come and see you, do we have a lot of immigrants from stupid city here in Zeb’s city only I have met some silly people today.”

“We may have there is a new law out that we have to welcome people from stupid city as friends of the crown like it or not.” The king replied.

“Oh is see I told his mother who just repeated the word why, all the time if he does not come to the castle the moment he gets home the king will send soldiers to kill him." The king burst out laughing.

"That should get his attention." The king laughed again just then the court caller entered and called out.

"Someone name Claude to see you sire."

"My word that was quick." The king "giggled send him in."

Claude entered very carefully "You wanted to see me your majesty?

"Yes Claude do you remember the story you told in the bakers shop about the piper and how he got rid of all those birds?

"Yes your majesty I do." Claude said.

"Well the story you told was the reason we got rid of the birds not because of the fair maiden but because of sing a song Sam, so for your information and getting rid of the birds I am giving you a bag of gold so you can buy your mother a new home, what do you say Claude?

"That is very kind of you your majesty but I won't buy my mother a new home she is alright where she is, I will buy me a new home and get me a fair damsel for my own and live with her."

"Fine Claude a man after my own heart spoken like a true gentleman, okay you go and see Silas my bank manager and he has the bag of gold meant for the piper but he did not have to come."

"Thank you your majesty I will leave you now." and he went out.

"Okay let's get this concert going"

*****

Came the night of the concert of the King and Him everyone had turned up the butcher the baker the candlestick maker was supposed to be there but no knew where he was, but there was rumor going around he had a new woman who was stringing him along, but he said candles needed string, anyway on with the cunning plan as I mentioned everyone was there the ones mentioned plus the Queen who was no relation to the king and the queens mother who used to be a wrestler in the circus, rumor had it the daughter was the referee .

People came from far and wide to see this famous

king play himself as no one else would, everything was set, even the queen”s makeup, the orchestra was all fired up but the fire department put them out.

All was quiet when the curtain rose (have you ever seen a curtain rose little red flower) anyway on with the show the curtain rose and fell to the ground as no one had fastened it up but no worries the king went on, and he went on and on and everyone was speechless including the king who just went on and on but nothing came out.

And just at the moment when it was the kings turn to sing and everyone expected a baritone”s voice out came a voice from another world, (the king wished it was) the king kept singing while Singasong Sam tried to put the words into the kings mouth, but had never thought of practicing beforehand, the king sang low while Sam sang high on account of his pants being too tight the audience never uttered a whisper (but a little titter ran through the house but no one caught it).

No one said a word because if they did the king would lock them in the castle prison and no one wanted that (because the bed"s here were too hard and the food even harder.)

When the king had finished, the audience gave him a standing ovation while sitting down as no one was going to do anything else were they because after all, he is the king.

*****

After the show, the king waited at the exit for everyone to come out of the theatre and to ask them how they enjoyed the show and to blow his own trumpet, as he was waiting for shaking hands with everyone who came out and saying.

"How did you like my show?"

"Wonderful, grovel marvelous creep excellent suck suck." And so on they came not wishing to upset the king in any way and anger him, until out walked a blind man, not knowing the king was asking the questions said.

"Who was that lead singer, he sounded as if his pants were too tight it was terrible and shocking." and words like that, the king was taken aback. (When we know he should have taken a front)

Never has anyone told the king the truth so he took the blind man to one side (he could have taken him to two sides, but it would have been no point he was blind) the king said to the blind man.

“Can you do trick’s and spells?

“No tried it once cut my finger off.”

“Pity I had a good job lined up for you, looks like I will have to keep Singasong my pants are too tight Sam on the books, but seeing as you are a truthful man you shall never want for anything ever again.”

“Can I have my sight back? The man asked.

“Don’t be ridiculous.” The king replied.

On with the story

The next morning the king sent for Sam and said to him.

“If you ever have another cunning plan, pray please keep it to yourself, your sorcery isn’t up to scratch your spells never work, and another thing your ears are too big plus you just cannot sing for toffee.”

*****

Sam was beside himself and thought he would have to do something very special and get back on the king's good side, (mind you his bad side was even worse) so Sam went to his room to think of something special he could do to please the king.

Meanwhile, Solengena was flying through the night on her red broomstick, as her brown one was in the broom garage for repair with the WBA (Witches Broom Association).

"I am feeling hungry." She said to herself (as no one else was there.)

"I will stop and have something to eat." She saw a bright light in the distance and flew down to take a look and saw it was a café and getting closer saw the café was called.

The coven café, known to the locals as (The Coven with the biggest oven) Solengena said to herself. (As no one else was there again)

"I will check it out it sounds like a good place to eat." MacDonald"s had not been invented yet.

Solengena parked her broom in the broom park and locked it and was walking towards the café when she was approached by a manacumber, for those who don't know what a manacumber is I will explain.

A manacumber is half man half cucumber, the man half is not bad, but the cucumber half is not a very pretty sight and a right load of green stuff, as he approached Solengena he was tossing his caterpillars in the air thinking he was some cool manacumber.

"Hey witchy woman spends a little time with me by the way, my name is Shirl." He said.

Solengena screamed (she hated the name shirl). "Listen to me green face why don't you go and boil your head."

This made the manacumber green with rage so he sloped away to boil his head, Solengena went inside the café and was surprised to find it was full of witches, goblins, and warlocks (men witches) she wanted something nice to eat and tried to catch the waiters eye, but he was showing off throwing it in the air trying to impress a girl witch.

The waiter came over after some time and said.

"What do you fancy, or would you rather eat." (Cheeky devil) Solengena thought they are all the same these devils.

Solengena was having a bit of trouble reading the menu, "I am having a bit of trouble reading this menu." She said.

"Try turning it up to the right way lady." The waiter said sneering.

"I would like to see the manager please?"

"Fat chance of you seeing the manager you cannot see the menu.

He replied sneering. (The sneering little devil isn't he.)

"Bring the manager." Solengena demanded. (Demanding isn't she).

Just then two strangers came through the door and there was an almighty crash, (they forgot to open the glass door)

The two strangers swaggered up to the counter the waitress said.

“Could I be off assistance strangers?” They knew she had been Myer trained.

“Yea can you get someone to get this glass out of my head?”

“Yes apart from that? The waitress asked.

“Yes, we want two teas and two bacon butties.” One of the strangers said.

Then he said. “How did you know we were strangers?”

“It”s the way you swaggered in all strangers swagger haven”t you seen John Wayne films.”

“Oh yes of course.” One stranger turned to his mate and said.

“Have you noticed all the witches?”

His friend replied. “Witches what witches.”

“There witches” “Where witches? “Over there witches”

Is mate said “How did you know they were witches.”

“The pointed hats on the table give them away.” He replied.

“Oh, yea never thought of that.” The other one said.

As you can tell the strangers are a bit stupid they probably come from a place called Stupid City where all the town and cities in the area send anyone stupid to Stupid City.

Anyway, the two strangers had their teas and bacon butties and left to return to Stupid City, the manager finally came over to see Solengena.

“Yes madam can I be of assistance?” He also had been Myer trained.

“Your waiter has been rude to me.” She said.

“Ignore him he comes from Stupid City could I suggest something.” The manager said with a faint smile.” (Solengena thought it was a smile but could have been wind.)

“Go and boil your head.” He said under his breath. “Oh yes I have to apologize for my staff it’s so hard to get good staff these days, anyway have to rush.” And he walked away with a swagger. (The swagger kept very close to him)

Solengena left and unlocked her broom and was just about to set off on it when the manager came rushing towards her screaming she had not paid the bill, just as he reached her she set off on her broom and gave him the brush off, and then turned him into a bacon buttie, off into the blue yonder she rose. (Have you ever seen a blue yonder rose small blue flower?)

Solengena Flew high above the land and sea towards Zeb's Windy City.

*****

Meanwhile in Zeb's windy city Singasong Sam was trying out some new tricks and potions he had just received from Demetelious the (Wait there is more merchant) came through the post took 28 days money-back guarantee, Sam did not mind the wait Demetelious lives in another town called 1800 city he seems to sell a lot of things of no good to anyone but people keep buying off him.

(Nowt as gullible as folk)

Anyway, Sam was trying out his new spells when

the king in a brand new coat came rushing in shouting.

“I have been stung, I have been stung.” (He had been stung twice)

“How much did they charge you? Sam asked.

“What are you talking about? The king replied.

“The coat, how much did they charge you for it? Sam said.

“Not the coat you blithering idiot I have been stung on the bum by something.” The king replied.

“Take your pants down and let’s have a look.” Sam said.

So the king took his pants down and shown Sam his bum, now also in the room at the time was the mayor of Zeb and the kings tailor who had made the kings coat the very same day, he had come to Sam to ask him for some advice about love and to make a love potion to give to Mrs. Shoots whose late husband made boots, Sam thought he will need more than a love potion more like a miracle, she has a face like a can of angry worms. Still loves blind so they say, maybe they can introduce her to the blind man.

Anyway, the king took down his pants and there on his bum was a big red wheel (maybe it came off a big red bike) Sam said.

"Someone is going to have to suck out the poison or you may die." They all looked at each other and the room was silent.

"Looks like you are going to die" Sam said. Then thought what if I sucked out the poison the king would be so grateful and would grant me anything. (Naw forget it he is going to die)

"I will try one of my new potions."

"Are they any good?" The king asks

"Demetelious swears by them, mind you he swears by everything, he sells." So Sam put the cream onto the king's bum and said.

"Make this cream cure the kings bum then he will become my chum." (No, I am not from Stupid City)

"It will take about twelve hours." Sam said.

“Twelve hours, what am I suppose to do for twelve hours.” The king asks.

“I don’t know have half a day off.” Sam replied.

The king went away muttering something under his breath none of them could catch like

“I will have them all beheaded or something boring like that if it doesn’t work.

Sam thought what if it doesn’t work I will have to flee the country, maybe I could go to Australia and become a politician I believe you don’t have to be very bright, but we will see.

The mayor, who was in the room also had come to see Sam about his bunions.

“I have heard onions are good for bunions then I have heard coal is good for moles, what can one do with all this daft advice.” The mayor said.

“First of all, don’t listen to it.” Sam replied.

(Maybe I can try the mole pellets I got from Demetelious let’s see first you dig a hole next to the mole's nest, oh damn wrong moles)

Then Sam decided to mix the mayor a potion of his making and handed it to him.

"Now put the cream on your moles three times a day and repeat after me, a mole in the hand is worth err two in a plastic bag, sorry I had no rhyme for bunions off you go then." Sam said to the mayor "Hope it works." Sam thought. "Fat chance"

"What is this for?" The mayor asked.

"That is for your moles." Sam replied.

"I haven"t got moles idiot I came to you about my bunions."

What can I do he will report me to the king for being stupid and you know what that means, yes a trip to the stupid city mind you if the king's potions don't work at least I will be safe from him, on second thought forget it.

"It's Altziemers." Sam said.

"Altziemers what about Altziemers" The mayor replied.

“I have a touch of it I have to go and see a very expensive specialist the best in the land so I have heard.”

“Sorry Sam, but what about my bunions.” The mayor looked at Sam.

“Wait a minute, if have a new very large book of spells I bought last year from a company called spellbound, now let me see.”

Sam got the very large spellbook by spellbound down from the shelf and opened it.

“Now let”s see bunions, it says here onions are good for bunions.”

“That is what I have heard and I am not walking around with my shoes full of smelly onions.” The mayor was getting angry.

“Are you going to help me or not or have I to report you to the king.” The mayor said.

“Okay, it”s cool, let”s see bunions, it says here if pain persists, see your doctor.”

“You idiot you are the doctor you ordering fool and I am here to see you.” The mayor said.

“That is a bit sharp, ordering fool I was only trying to help.”

“What are you going to do Sam.” the mayor looked at Sam very angrily.

“Okay, take this cream it is supposed to be very good, Demetelious swears by it.”

The mayor took it off Sam and was leaving and said something under his breath Sam could not catch like. (I hope he gets his head chopped off) or something boring trivial like that.

Back at the Coven with the biggest oven, all the staff wondered where the manager had gone, and then the waitress said to the waiter.

“Where is the manager?”

“I don’t know I haven”t seen him for some time since he went out after that witch”

“What witch?” (Don’t start that again)

“You know the one who never paid.”

“Oh her”

"I will go and see if he is outside." Off the waiter went to see if he could find the manager as he got outside, he screamed and shriveled up, no one knew he was a vampire. (Just kidding threw that in to see if you were paying attention).

The waiter looked all around and no manager could be found only a bacon buttie lying on the floor.

"Strange who would leave a bacon buttie outside and picked it up." The then went inside the café.

"Was he there?" The waitress asked.

"No, I just found this bacon buttie." The waiter replied.

"Give it to the dog." So the waiter threw the dog the bacon buttie which he ate with gusto.

*****

Solengena landed in the Zeb's windy city and parked her broom in the broom park and locked it, and went to find Singasong Sam the sorcerer man; she stopped a stranger and said.

"Hello, stranger, could you tell me where I can find Singasong Sam the sorcerer man."

“How did you know I was a stranger?” He asked.

“It”s because you swaggered” She replies.

“Well, if I am a stranger, I don’t know where this Singasong Sam is will I. and with that walked away.

“I will bet he is from Stupid City.” Solengena said and walked on.

The next stop was the boot shop owned by Mrs. Shoots.

“Could you tell me where I can find Singasong Sam the sorcerer man?” Solengena asked.

“Yes, he is in the king’s castle, but be aware the king is not very well he has been stung.” Mrs. Shoots said.

“How much did they charge him?” Solengena asked.

“What.” Mrs. Shoots replied.

“How much did it cost him?” Solengena asked once again.

"Not that kind of stung, stung by something." Mrs. Shoots replied very puzzled.

"Stung on his bum, very painful I heard it through the grapevine."

"Did Marvin Gaye tell you?" Solengena said.

"Who is Marvin Gaye Mrs. Shoot"s looked at Solengena.

"Never mind, I will find this Sorcerer." She walked out of the shop and towards the king"s castle where she was stopped by the security guard.

"What do you want?" He asked.

"I have traveled a long way and need to see the sorcerer Singasong Sam."

"No one sees the king"s sorcerer without an appointment" The guard said.

"Please, I have traveled far and need to see him urgently." Solengena tried her womanly charm but it did not work.

"Yea so you say but orders are orders, so push off witchy woman."

What a rude man, but then she thought, I will fly over on my broom, so off she went and got her broom from the broom park paid her fee and got on her broom and flew over the castle walls the security man saw her but could do nothing. From the smell of potions, she found the sorcerer's room and flew onto the patio and went inside.

Sam was busy reading his very big spellbook from the company spellbound and did not hear Solengena come in he turned around and it gave him a bit of a scare.

"Who are you?" he asked.

"My name is Solengena the witch I come from a land far away called Faraway land." She replied.

"And what brings you to Zeb's windy city." Sam asks.

"I have come to see you as you are supposed to be the best brain in the land, and only you can help me."

"And how can I help you Solengena?" Sam asked.

So Solengena told Sam the story of how she was

named after a plant and wanted so much to change it as she hated being named after a mere plant.

“Can I show you something?” Sam said.

“Yes, but beware I am a witch.” Sam just smiled and went to a bookcase and brought out a gardening book on rare flowers and opened it.

“Have you seen the plant you are named after?” Sam asked.

“No, I have not.” Solengena replied and Sam gave her the book and when Solengena looked at the plant it took her breath away.

“Why would anyone who was named after something so beautiful want to change her name to something boring?”

Solengena looked at Sam and Sam looked at Solengena and it was love at first sight.

“Will you marry me?” Sam asked.

Solengena said yes and they held each other.

“The only thing in the way is I have a few problems.” Sam said.

“Go on, you are already married.” Solengena replied.

“No spell problems.”

Sam told Solengena about the spells he hoped would work and about the king”s stings and the mayor”s bunions.

“I heard about it from Mrs. Shoots.” Solengena said.

“And that is another problem and then there is the tailor and if you want a husband with no head, I had better come up with something and fast.”

“Never mind my love together we can do anything and I will help you.”

"Come Solengena the game is afoot.” Sam laughed.

So Sam and Solengena cured the king the mayor could walk again the tailor and Mrs. shoots got married and now make suits to go with the boots the blind man was best man but could not see anything and they all lived happily ever after.

As for the café, the waiter married the waitress and bought the lease on the café and the dog thinks it is the manager.

The end